THE PLAYBOOK

52 Rules to Aim, Shoot, and Score in This Game Called Life

BY KWAME ALEXANDER

PHOTOGRAPHS BY THAI NEAVE

Clarion Books
An Imprint of HarperCollins*Publishers*

• • • • • • With special thanks to • • • • • • •

JoEllen McCarthy, Aditya Kalia, Mary Rand Hess,
Trenton Hess, Castleton Elementary, Singapore American School,
Sid Reischer, and Angela Turnbull.

Clarion Books is an imprint of HarperCollins Publishers.

The Playbook
Text copyright © 2017 by Kwame Alexander
Photos copyright © 2017 by Thai Neave

ISBN 978-0-06-328877-5

Typography by Lisa Vega
22 23 24 25 26 LBC 5 4 3 2 1

First paperback edition, 2023

IMAGE CREDITS:

Page(s) i: © Shutterstock; **1–2**: © Thai Neave; **5**: © Shutterstock; **7**: © Getty Images; **11**: © Shutter-
stock; **12–13**: © Thai Neave; **14**: © Shutterstock; **18–21**: © Thai Neave; **22**: © Shutterstock; **25–27**:
© Thai Neave; **28–29**: © Shutterstock (ball), Getty Images (hand); **30–31**: © Getty Images (texture),
Shutterstock (figure); **32–35**: © Thai Neave; **36–37**: © Shutterstock; **38–41**: © Thai Neave; **42–43**: ©
Shutterstock; **45–47**: © Thai Neave; **48–49**: © Shutterstock; **50**: © Getty Images; **53**: © Getty Images;
57: © Shutterstock; **58–61**: © Thai Neave; **62, 65**: Shutterstock (ball); **66–67**: © Thai Neave; **69**: ©
Getty Images; **70–71**: © Shutterstock (line art); **71–73**: © Thai Neave; **74–75, 77**: © Shutterstock;
78–79: © Thai Neave; **80–81**: © Shutterstock; **82–85**: © Thai Neave; **86**: Shutterstock (ball); **88–89**:
© Shutterstock; **92–93**: © Thai Neave; **97**: © Shutterstock; **100–101**: © Thai Neave; **102**: Shutterstock
(ball); **103–5**: © Thai Neave; **106**: © Shutterstock (line art); **108–11**: © Thai Neave; **112–13**: © Getty
Images (texture), Thai Neave (photo); **116–17**: © Thai Neave; **119–21**: © Shutterstock; **122–23**: ©
Thai Neave; **124–25**: © Getty Images; **126–27**: © Thai Neave; **129–30**: © Shutterstock (ball); **134–35**:
© Dreamstime; **136–37**: © Thai Neave; **139–41**: © Shutterstock; **142–43**: © Thai Neave; **144–45**:
© Shutterstock; **146–47**: Getty Images (texture); **148–50**: © Shutterstock (line art); **150–51**: © Thai
Neave; **152–53**: © Shutterstock; **154–55**: © Thai Neave; **156–57**: © Shutterstock; **158–61**: © Thai
Neave; **162–63, 169**: © Shutterstock.

For Cedric Howard, the best teammate ever
• • • • • • • • *and* • • • • • • • •
Margaret Raymo, the best coach in the game

Warm-up: The Rules

Sports teaches you character, it teaches you to play by the rules, it teaches you to know what it feels like to win and lose—it teaches you about life.

—BILLIE JEAN KING, Hall of Fame thirty-nine-time Grand Slam tennis champion, founder of the Women's Tennis Association

In 1891, when James Naismith invented the game of basketball with a soccer ball and two peach baskets to use as goals, he also had to create some rules—13 of them in fact. Rules like:

THE BALL MAY BE THROWN IN ANY DIRECTION WITH ONE OR BOTH HANDS AND THE TIME SHALL BE TWO 15-MINUTE HALVES WITH FIVE MINUTES' REST BETWEEN.

Over the next 100-plus years, these rules would govern the hoops game and make basketball one of the most popular sports in the world.

I believe that sports are a great metaphor for life. In our games, we decide who the best players are to assist us, we flex our skills, and we test our will to win on and off the court. Our character is built during the times we are victorious and also during the times we are met with major challenges. This is when we find out what we're really made of. There are countless stories of athletes who faced defeat to accomplish historic feats. They, like you and me, had dreams. Big dreams. How do we make our dreams come true? I believe that we have to be passionate, determined, focused, and work hard, in order to succeed. But, we also have to master the rules of the game.

WANT TO BE A BALLER, KNOW THE RULES.

WANT TO DO BETTER IN SCHOOL, KNOW THE RULES.

WANT TO HAVE BETTER FRIENDSHIPS, KNOW THE RULES.

WANT TO SUCCEED IN THE GAME OF LIFE, KNOW THE RULES.

In eighth grade, I was eager to succeed. In sports and in popularity. I wanted people to know who I was, especially the girls. I wanted to walk down the halls and get *high-fives*, *daps*, and *hollas*. I wanted to be cool. I wanted to be *Da Man!* Thing was, I had no idea how to do it. Until a friend named Vince suggested basketball. I was tall and agile and my dad had been a star baller, so I figured what I lacked in actual talent, my genes would make up for. I tried out and made the team.

First game of the season, I bring the ball up the court, dribble the ball between my legs, behind my back, no defender in sight. I get to the half-court line and decide, in front of hundreds of classmates, teachers, parents . . . and girls, that I'm going to shoot, and hopefully score the first points of the game. I throw the ball up right there at the half-court line. It's the first play of the season, and if I make this, there will be newspaper clippings of me for my kids to read one day. If I make it, everyone will know *Kwame Alexander*.

I don't make it.

The ball goes over the backboard and hits the scoreboard. Me and my coolness get benched. So much for basketball. I finish out the season sitting mostly on the sidelines. One of the rules I'd learned growing up was to **never give up,** especially when you really want something. So, the following year—my freshman year—I try out for the junior varsity team.

I don't make it.

Cedric, my best friend, who was not as tall as I was, but ripped—he had muscles, y'all—suggested that we try out for the football team, because *everybody liked football players.* I said **yes!** We both made the team. Wide receivers.

First game of the season, he gallops down one sideline, I speed down the other. I eagerly await my chance to get the ball, **score,** hear the cheers. I see my mom in the stands, so I wave at her. The quarterback looks my way. Oh yes, it's about to go down. I'm about to score a **touchdown**—then everyone will know me. Thing is, I never get the ball. I get knocked flat on my butt by some monster whose actual nickname is, get this, "Monster." Lights out. *Crickets.* Cedric goes on to score many touchdowns as the star receiver of our football team. He even plays in college. My mom benches me after the hit. And it's no more football for me. Truth was, football wasn't really an interest of mine. I thought it might make me cool, but all it made me was sore. I guess the rule I learned that day was know your strengths, know your passion, know that if your heart isn't in it, the Monster will hurt you!

Then my mom suggests another sport. *Kwame, cool is what you make it,* I remember her saying. *If you're bent on playing a sport, why don't you try tennis?*

Tennis? The *uncoolest* sport on earth. My dad had played high school tennis too. He was a high school competitor of Arthur Ashe—the one exception to the *tennis isn't cool* rule. I thought my mom was bonkers. No way I was going to sport a pair of white shorts and an aluminum racket. Thing was, I trusted my mom. She was pretty smart and always had my back. She took me out to the courts, taught me some of the basics, practiced with me. I decided to give it a shot.

SOMETIMES, YOU MAY NOT AGREE WITH OR UNDERSTAND THE ADVICE YOU GET, BUT IF YOU HEED IT, IT JUST MIGHT STICK WITH YOU UNTIL YOU COME TO UNDERSTAND IT.

Until you live it and breathe it! But first you need to *say yes* to the possibility. You need to be open to new things. You have to *say yes* to yourself. The most important rule I think I've ever learned is that when you're presented with an opportunity that may seem different or challenging or unknown, sometimes you've got to summon the courage to trust yourself and SAY YES!

So, I said YES!

I tried out for the tennis team and made it. I was number twelve. On a roster of twelve. My father had purchased me a gold-plated tennis racket from K-mart to go along with my corduroy shorts and red Chuck Taylors. I looked nothing like a tennis player, and played even worse. Actually, I didn't play in one match that first year. I just watched. The next season, I moved up to number nine, and I got to play in my first match, which I won. Suddenly, my confidence was building, but my ego wasn't. I wanted to be a starter on the team, to play in every match, and that motivated me to keep playing, to keep trying, even when faced with the ridicule of some of my teammates. The older guys on the team didn't think I was that good, didn't think I was worthy to be a starter, and didn't take me seriously. So, I devised a plan. It involved practice. And more practice. And still, even more practice. Six hours every day during summer vacation, we practiced: Me and Shawn and Rob and Paul. And Claudia—the real reason I wanted to be cool.

We all have what it takes to do exactly what we want to do in life, no matter what anyone else says. If someone tells you, "You can't do this because you are [fill in the blank]," I say embrace the challenge. Wear it like a new pair of Converse or Jordans. Meet it head-on. Find your grit and put in the work to elevate your game.

CHAMPIONS TRAIN, CHUMPS COMPLAIN.

Be true to your unique, amazing, and awesome self. Motivate yourself, and powerfully step into your dreams to create the life you want, and do not let anyone or anything stop you!

PRACTICE. WORK HARD. FOCUS. PREPARE YOURSELF FOR THE THING THAT YOU WANT TO **ACCOMPLISH**—ACE A TEST, MAKE A TEAM, JOIN A CLUB, GO TO COLLEGE—WHATEVER IT IS, YOU SIMPLY MUST PUT. IN. THE. **WORK.** . . . . .

The next year, I was number four on the team. My dedication had paid off. I played in every match. I won every one. In the district tournament, the number one, two, and three seeds on our team all got beat. Guess who made it to the finals? Yep, ME! All because I said yes. All of a sudden, I felt cool. I had overcome a few challenges and succeeded beyond my wildest dreams. Of course, you want to know if I won . . . stay tuned.

The Playbook is a collection of short poems, divided into 4 quarters of 13 rules each, accompanied by uplifting quotes from famous people who have overcome challenges to achieve amazing things. They have each found their path to greatness.

Whether you're playing soccer or tennis, baseball or lacrosse, softball or basketball, you've got to find the right motivation and creativity to propel you to success. Think of *The Playbook* as a source of inspiration: *52 rules to aim, shoot, and score in this game called life.* Like James Naismith's, these are my rules, for basketball, for sports, and for life!

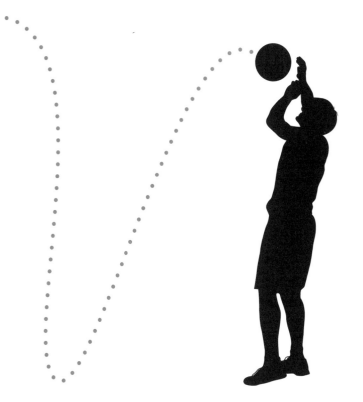

1st Quarter

Grit

Grit *(noun)*:

courage and resolve;

strength of character.

In eighth grade, I had to do a book report, and I waited, as usual, until the very last minute. My house was pretty much a library, so I grabbed the first slim volume I saw off the shelf in our family room. It was a book about Wilma Rudolph, an Olympic track champion. It took me about an hour to read the book. Her story was remarkable. What I found out about her life changed mine.

When she was born, Wilma Rudolph weighed only four and a half pounds, and she spent the first eleven years of her childhood fighting illnesses such as scarlet fever, whooping cough, double pneumonia, and, get this, polio. Polio causes paralysis and has no cure. So, left with only one working leg, Wilma was fitted with a metal leg brace at around age five.

Every week, she and her mom took a Greyhound bus from their small town to Nashville, Tennessee, for her physical therapy, so that she could learn to walk with her brace. During these trips, Wilma witnessed and experienced the segregation of the Deep South—they always had to ride in the back of the bus, and they couldn't eat in most restaurants. Witnessing racial divides and experiencing her own disability gave Wilma grit and determination that would help her overcome some pretty huge challenges.

Often, Wilma would try to remove her leg brace so she could play like her friends and siblings. By age eleven, she finally kicked off that leg brace permanently and began practicing to walk, run, and play ball. It was painful and hard, but she was determined. Her brothers set up a basketball hoop in their yard, where she played every chance she got. After years and years of hard work and sheer willpower, she could not only walk well, but she could run faster than most kids. She became a star basketball player at her school, where Coach C. C. Gray gave her the nickname "Skeeter" because she was so fast. Imagine that: a girl who walked in special shoes with a leg brace for years was now given a nickname because of her speed.

Wilma became an all-state basketball player, setting the state record of forty-nine points in a single game. She was gifted, so gifted that word soon reached Ed Temple, track coach at Tennessee State University, who recruited her to start training with his team. Surprisingly, she qualified for the 1956 Olympic Games in Melbourne, Australia, where she became the youngest member of the U.S. track team at just sixteen years old. She flew home with a bronze medal.

After high school, Wilma went to Tennessee State, where she studied education and trained for the next Olympic Games. Within four years, she was back at the Olympics, this time in Rome, Italy, where she set world records in the 100-meter dash, 200-meter dash, and the 100-meter relay. The Olympics were a huge success and a game changer for Wilma, as she became the first American woman to win three gold medals in a single Olympics. She was soon known as the world's fastest woman.

She was later inducted into the U.S. Olympic Hall of Fame and founded the Wilma Rudolph Foundation to help inspire and encourage amateur athletics. Not bad for a girl whose doctors said she would always have trouble walking.

When I presented my book report to the class, I ended by saying that we all face challenges and defeats in our life, but if you are self-determined and committed to putting in the work, you can bounce back like Wilma Rudolph did. I got an $A+$ on the report, but more important, I realized that if she could overcome a paralyzed leg and become a track star, then I could work hard and excel in whatever sport I chose—and, perhaps, in life.

Rule #1

IT TAKES SKILL
TO MAKE
THE LAST SHOT,
BUT IT TAKES CONFIDENCE
TO TAKE IT.

I have missed more than 9,000 shots in my career. I have lost almost 300 games. On 26 occasions I have been entrusted to take the game-winning shot and missed. And I have failed over and over and over again in my life. And that is why I succeed.

—Michael Jordan, six-time NBA champion with the Chicago Bulls, five-time MVP

WHEN THE GAME IS ON
THE LINE,
DON'T FEAR.

GRAB THE BALL.

TAKE IT
TO THE HOOP.

I don't focus on what I'm up against. I focus on my goals and I try to ignore the rest.

—Venus Williams, seven-time Grand Slam tennis champion, Olympic gold medalist

THE SIZE OF YOUR HEART MATTERS MORE THAN THE SIZE OF YOUR OPPONENT.

It's not how big you are, it's how big you play.

—John Wooden, ten-time NCAA championship—
winning coach with UCLA and six-time national
coach of the year

The fight is won . . . behind the lines, in the gym, and out there on the road, long before I dance under those lights.

—Muhammad Ali, "The Greatest" world heavyweight boxing champion, philanthropist, social activist

PRACTICE
PREPARES YOU
FOR THAT GLORIOUS MOMENT
WHEN YOU HOLD
THE BALL
AND DESTINY
IN YOUR HANDS.

27

LEARN THE FUNDAMENTALS,
SO YOU CAN ALWAYS
BE IN A POSITION

TO DRIBBLE
PASS
OR SHOOT.

28

WHEN THE BALL
IS IN YOUR HANDS,
BE A TRIPLE TRIPLE TRIPLE
THREAT.

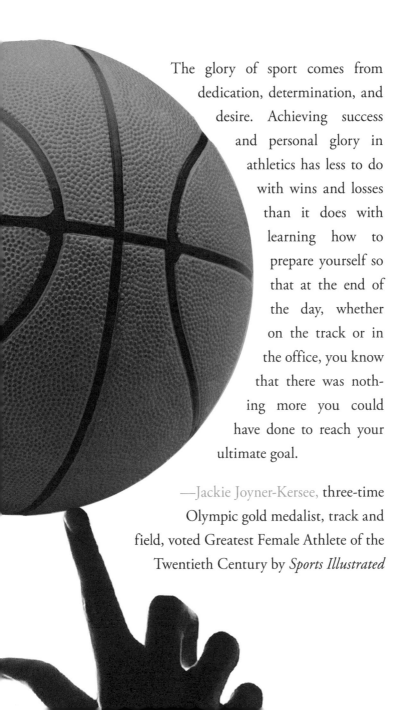

The glory of sport comes from dedication, determination, and desire. Achieving success and personal glory in athletics has less to do with wins and losses than it does with learning how to prepare yourself so that at the end of the day, whether on the track or in the office, you know that there was nothing more you could have done to reach your ultimate goal.

—Jackie Joyner-Kersee, **three-time** Olympic gold medalist, track and field, voted Greatest Female Athlete of the Twentieth Century by *Sports Illustrated*

PRACTICE
IS SO ROUTINE
AND SOMETIMES
ROUTINES ARE BORING.
BUT IF YOU DON'T PRACTICE
YOU WILL GET BEAT
ROUTINELY.

30

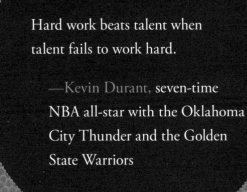

Hard work beats talent when
talent fails to work hard.

—Kevin Durant, seven-time
NBA all-star with the Oklahoma
City Thunder and the Golden
State Warriors

32

If you've given the greatest effort that you can expect from yourself, then you'll always get what you deserve.

–C. Vivian Stringer, Hall of Fame basketball coach, and assistant coach of the 2004 women's basketball Olympic team

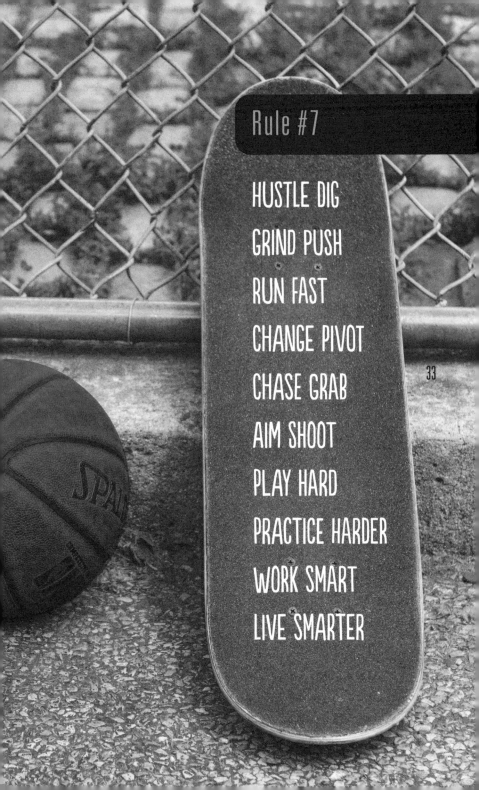

HUSTLE DIG

GRIND PUSH

RUN FAST

CHANGE PIVOT

CHASE GRAB

AIM SHOOT

PLAY HARD

PRACTICE HARDER

WORK SMART

LIVE SMARTER

33

I just keep fighting and try to be the last one standing.

—Li Na, French Open and Australian Open tennis champion

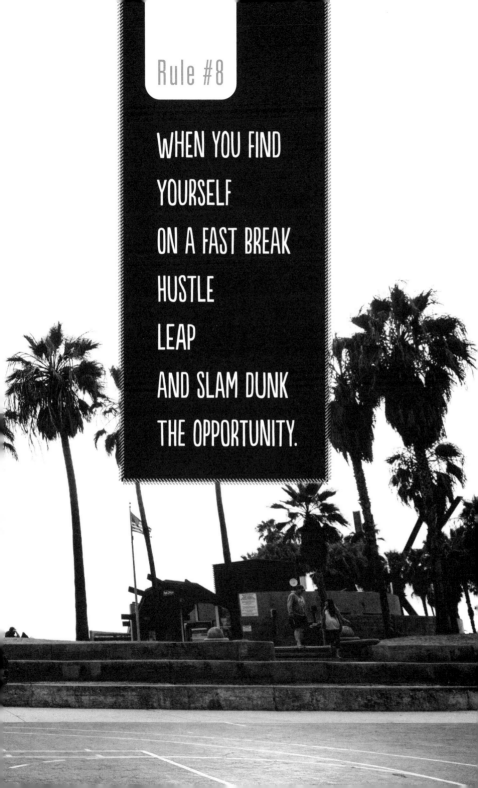

Rule #8

WHEN YOU FIND
YOURSELF
ON A FAST BREAK
HUSTLE
LEAP
AND SLAM DUNK
THE OPPORTUNITY.

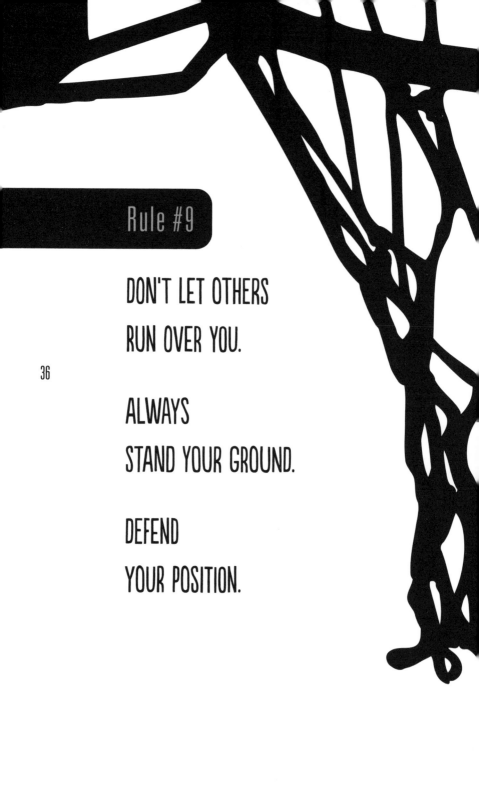

Rule #9

DON'T LET OTHERS
RUN OVER YOU.

36

ALWAYS
STAND YOUR GROUND.

DEFEND
YOUR POSITION.

I've worked too hard and too long to let anything stand in the way of my goals. I will not let my teammates down and I will not let myself down.

—Mia Hamm, two-time Olympic gold medalist and FIFA Women's World Cup champion

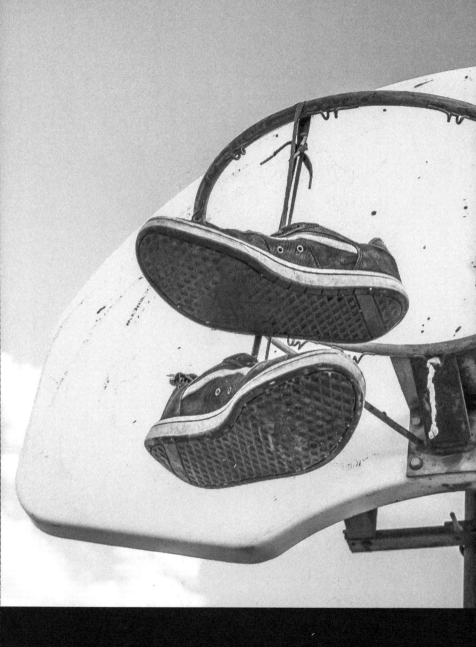

Success is no accident. It is hard work, perseverance, learning, studying, sacrifice, and, most of all, love of what you are doing or learning to do.

WHEN YOU STOP PLAYING *YOUR* GAME YOU'VE ALREADY LOST.

—Pelé, three-time FIFA World Cup champion with Brazil, most successful league goal scorer (541) in the world

There's winning and there's losing, and in life you have to know they both will happen. But what's never acceptable to me is quitting.

—Magic Johnson, five-time NBA champion with the Los Angeles Lakers, successful American businessman

Rule #11

DON'T LET PAST MISTAKES
STOP YOU FROM PLAYING
THE CURRENT GAME.

PUT YOUR FULL HEART
PURE PASSION
UNSTOPPABLE FAITH

ON THE LINE
AS IF YOU'VE NEVER HIT
THE COURT BEFORE.

YOU CAN ALWAYS

DO BETTER THAN YOU DID
WORK HARDER THAN YOU WORKED
LEAP BROADER THAN YOU LEAPT

SO

DIG DEEPER
CLAW HARDER
REBOUND BETTER

THAN EVER BEFORE.

There may be people who have
more talent than you, but there's
no excuse for anyone to work harder than you do.

—Derek Jeter, five-time MLB World Series
champion with the New York Yankees

FIND GRIT
WHEN YOU WANT TO
QUIT

COOLNESS
WHEN YOU GET
HEATED

AND DETERMINATION
WHEN YOU FEEL
DEFEATED.

Winning is great, sure, but if you are really going to do something in life, the secret is learning how to lose. Nobody goes undefeated all the time. If you can pick up after a crushing defeat and go on to win again, you are going to be a champion someday.

—Wilma Rudolph, three-time Olympic gold medalist, track and field

45

2nd Quarter

Motiv

Motivation *(noun):* the desire or willingness of someone to do something.

50

Before I was born, my father was a star basketball and tennis player. They called him "Big Al." I remember looking through his photo albums and seeing newspaper clippings of his prowess on the court. His jump shot was sick. His serve-and-volley was lethal. His rebounding skills were *nasty*. And the pictures of him holding the championship trophies—in tennis and basketball—were inspiring to a young, budding athlete. I wanted trophies of my own. I wanted some of that cool.

All great players have to begin somewhere and must find the motivation deep inside of them to work harder, play harder, and win with heart. For me, it was wanting to be like my dad. For my favorite baller, LeBron James, who didn't have a father around to inspire him, it was something else.

LeBron James was born in 1984 in Akron, Ohio, to a teen mother, who raised him alone. He's talked about how his father not being in his life affected him, motivated him:

"Dad, you know what? I don't know you. I have no idea who you are. . . . The fuel that I use today—you not being there—it's part of the reason I grew up to become who I am. It's part of the reason why I want to be hands-on with my endeavors."

His mother struggled to find steady jobs, and the family moved from housing project to housing project. Growing up, James faced all the adversity that comes with living in impoverished conditions. When LeBron was nine years old, his mother made a life-changing decision to give her son a better chance at success. She let LeBron move in with his local football coach. It was in his new home that LeBron quickly found an outlet for his dreams and hopes—basketball. He excelled in AAU (Amateur Athletic Union) basketball as a middle school student, and a few years later led his high school team—composed of many of his Akron friends with whom he played AAU—to three straight championships. By his senior year, LeBron was named Gatorade National Player of the Year. In 2003, the same year he graduated high school, James made a decision to enter the NBA draft, where he became the number one pick for, get this, his hometown Cleveland Cavaliers.

The first seven years of his NBA career were met with praise—he lived up to the ball-handling, passing, and dunking skills that were characteristic of his stellar high school career. There was also heavy skepticism—could The King ever live up to the comparisons to His Airness, Michael Jordan? Did he possess the skill and will to win a championship or two? Would Ohio's Mr. Basketball reverse Cleveland's fifty-two-year sports curse? Cleveland, Ohio, has three major sports teams: the Cleveland Browns of the NFL, the Cleveland Indians of the MLB, and the Cleveland Cavaliers of the NBA. None of these teams had won a championship in 147 seasons, since 1964 when the Browns won the NFL championship.

In 2010, when he left Cleveland and joined the Miami Heat, the naysayers and haters multiplied, with many people—in Cleveland and beyond—insisting that he would never win a championship because 1) he wasn't a clutch player like Michael Jordan, and, more significantly, 2) he'd betrayed his hometown. It didn't matter that he remained committed to Ohio in general and Cleveland and Akron in particular, as evidenced by the $41 million he pledged to provide scholarships to students in Akron who grew up in challenging environments like he had. The city where he grew up and honed his skills, on and off the court, didn't care that he still considered himself one of them. They now saw him as the enemy.

Motivation can come from inspiration and encouragement, but it can also come from opposition and discouragement. LeBron took the good with the bad, used it as the driving force for the next four years of his career. He won back-to-back

NBA championships as a member of the Miami Heat. While his game elevated and his championship rings increased, the Cleveland Cavaliers got worse, with one losing season after another. And then, in 2014, LeBron surprised everyone. He left Miami and went back to, get this, Cleveland. The impetus for this decision: He wanted to bring a championship to his hometown.

Of course, those who were angry with him for leaving Cleveland in the first place were now his biggest fans and supporters. The King had come home. In his first year back, he led his team to the NBA Finals, but was beaten pretty handily by the incredibly shooting Golden State Warriors in six games. After the win, fans and media anointed the Warriors star Stephen Curry as one of the best players in the league. And when the next season came around and Golden State won seventy-three games—a new NBA record—Steph Curry was now considered *the best player* in the league. All of a sudden, the boy from Cleveland, who had been a star since middle school, who had carried teams on his back all the way to the Finals six straight years, was being surpassed by "the new face of the NBA."

In that next season, the Cavaliers again made it to the Finals, where they faced the Golden State Warriors. With a 3-1 deficit, staring defeat in the face, LeBron dug deep. Critics said the series was over, that no other team in the history of the NBA had ever come back and won a championship after being down like this, that LeBron's leadership had failed the team again and that the Warriors would repeat. In games five and six, LeBron scored 41 points each to force a 3-3 tie. In a nail-biting game seven, he hustled, scored, defended, and played the best game of his life to overcome adversity and lead the Cavaliers to what has been called the greatest comeback victory in the sports history.

He was determined to silence all the critics and prove the doubters wrong. He was driven, beyond what many thought was humanly possible, by the desire to, after a fifty-two-year sports curse, bring a championship to the city of Cleveland. Skill is something you can learn. Will is something you earn over time, by overcoming challenges. LeBron James has faced challenges on and off the court, and used those experiences to motivate himself beyond compare, to become perhaps the greatest player in NBA history.

58

NEVER LET ANYONE LOWER YOUR GOALS. OTHERS' EXPECTATIONS OF YOU ARE DETERMINED BY THEIR LIMITATIONS OF LIFE. THE SKY IS YOUR LIMIT. ALWAYS SHOOT FOR THE SUN AND YOU *WILL* SHINE.

I'll always be number 1 to myself.

—Moses Malone, three-time NBA MVP
and NBA champion with the
Philadelphia 76ers

SUCCESS COMES FROM
FACING FEAR,
OVERCOMING OBSTACLES,
WORKING HARD,
AND BELIEVING
YOU'RE GOOD
ENOUGH TO
WIN.

60

Luck has nothing to do with it, because I have spent many, many hours, countless hours, on the court working for my one moment in time, not knowing when it would come.

—Serena Williams, number one world tennis player (ATP rankings), twenty-one-time Grand Slam tennis champion

Rule #16

YOU MAY NOT BE

A STARTER

BUT ALWAYS

62

BE A STAR

IN YOUR MIND

READY TO SHINE

AT ANY TIME.

63

I want to make sure that I'm a shining light, or bringing life to every situation I'm in.

—Maya Moore, WNBA player for the Minnesota Lynx

SOMETIMES, WE NEED
OTHERS
TO MOTIVATE US
TO HELP US DREAM
TO BOUNCE IDEAS OFF
REBOUND WITH
GROW WITH.

A TEAM.
A DREAM TEAM.

64

No matter what accomplishments you make,
somebody helped you.

—Althea Gibson, **eleven-time Grand Slam
tennis champion**

STUDY THE PLANNING,
PATH, AND PERFORMANCE
OF THE GREAT ONES
WHO PLAYED
BEFORE YOU
SO YOU CAN "PICK UP"
THE THINGS
THAT WORKED
AND "PASS"
ON THE THINGS
THAT DIDN'T.

Champions behave like champions before they are champions.

—Bill Walsh, three-time NFL Super Bowl champion coach of the San Francisco 49ers

WHEN YOU'RE HOT, SHOOT. WHEN YOU'RE NOT, PASS. CHAMPIONS HIDE THEIR WEAKNESSES WITH THEIR STRENGTHS.

Start where you are. Use what you have. Do what you can.

—Arthur Ashe, **number one world tennis player (ATP rankings), winner of three Grand Slam titles**

A GOOD COACH LEADS THE TEAM.

A GREAT COACH CREATES LEADERS.

You can't force your will on people. If you want them to act differently, you need to inspire them to change themselves.

—Phil Jackson, **eleven-time NBA championship–winning coach with the Chicago Bulls and the Los Angeles Lakers**

KNOW THE COURT
KNOW WHERE TO GO
WHERE TO BE
FIND THE OPEN SPOT
BE IN THE RIGHT PLACE
AT THE RIGHT TIME
TO CREATE
YOUR BEST SHOT
FOR GREATNESS

Never underestimate the power of dreams and the influence of the human spirit. We are all the same in this notion: the potential for greatness lives within each of us.

—Wilma Rudolph, three-time Olympic gold medalist, track and field

EVEN IF
YOU'RE AFRAID,
WHEN YOU GET THE CHANCE
TO SHOOT,
LAUNCH
YOUR BEST
SHOT.

74

If you're afraid to fail, then you're probably going to fail.

—Kobe Bryant, five-time NBA champion with the Los Angeles Lakers

75

AT JUMP BALL
WHEN THE GAME BEGINS
BE ON YOUR TOES.
BE PREPARED
MENTALLY
AND PHYSICALLY
TO TAKE
THE LEAP.

Practice creates confidence.
Confidence empowers you.

—Simone Biles, four-time
Olympic gold medalist,
gymnastics

77

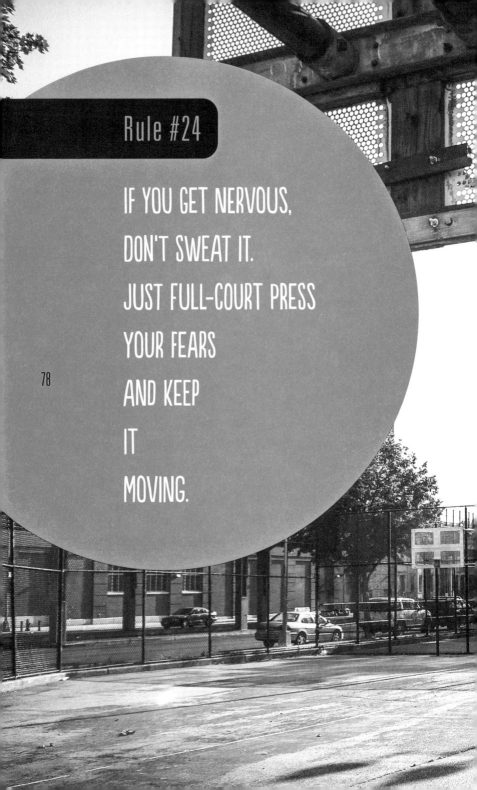

IF YOU GET NERVOUS,
DON'T SWEAT IT.
JUST FULL-COURT PRESS
YOUR FEARS
AND KEEP
IT
MOVING.

78

Never let the fear of striking out get in your way.

—Babe Ruth, seven-time World Series champion with the New York Yankees and the Boston Red Sox

IN THE FACE OF OPPOSITION, A WELL-TIMED CROSSOVER

Make it work no matter what you have to work with—that's something that stuck with me very early on as a point guard. Adjust. Get creative. Try a different angle, a different lane,

JUST MIGHT
GIVE YOU
ENOUGH SPACE
TO EXECUTE
THE PLAY
AND SCORE.

a different move or a different shot—just make it work.
—Stephen Curry, NBA champion, two-time MVP
with the Golden State Warriors

IN THIS GAME OF LIFE
YOUR FAMILY IS THE COURT
AND THE BALL IS YOUR HEART.
NO MATTER HOW GOOD YOU ARE,

82

NO MATTER HOW DOWN YOU GET, ALWAYS LEAVE YOUR HEART ON THE COURT.

All I ever wanted really, and continue to want out of life, is to give 100 percent to whatever I'm doing and to be committed to whatever I'm doing and then let the results speak for themselves. Also, to never take myself or people for granted and always be thankful and grateful to the people who helped me.

—Jackie Joyner-Kersee, three-time Olympic gold medalist in track and field, voted Greatest Female Athlete of the Twentieth Century by *Sports Illustrated*

Halftime

Ras

Passion

(noun):
a strong feeling of enthusiasm or excitement for something or about doing something.

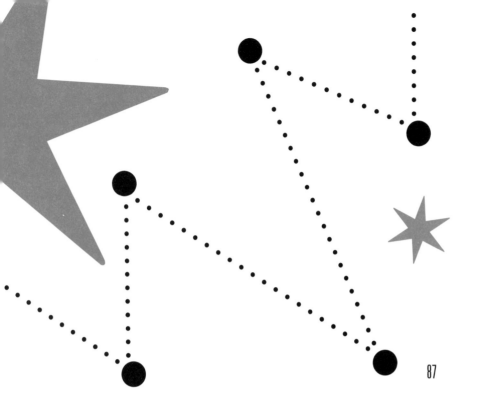

So having made it to the district tournament finals my junior year, I gave it my all. My parents came to the match. All my friends came.

And, I lost.

Losing is a test none of us has studied for. It's one of the hardest things to deal with in our young lives. Especially in the finals. But here's the thing: It's as much a part of life as winning, and true champions are resilient and learn how to rebound. To most of my friends, basketball and football were surefire ways to get noticed, to become cool, to be somebody. Basketball and football didn't work out, but I rebounded. I found my own path, and it worked for me. And while losing in the finals was almost unbearable, it was just a setback. Like the famous motivational speaker Willie Jolley says,

A SETBACK IS A SETUP
FOR A COMEBACK.

I got right back out on the court to perfect my game. The summer before my senior year in high school, I played tennis nine, ten hours a day. I took more lessons. And I loved every minute of it. My parents were working, and my friends didn't feel like driving way out to my house to pick me up, so I'd take two buses to the courts, a few times even walking the five miles to serve and volley under the summer sun. I did this because I loved playing tennis. It's what I dreamed about at night. It's what I watched on television when it rained. It's what I thought about while I cut the grass. It's what I did every day. And night. It was, quite simply, my passion.

I played numerous tournaments during the summer and

fall, and came in first place more than ten times. There was a collection of trophies sitting in my room that I was quite proud of. When the spring came and the season started, I found myself the number one seed on my high school tennis team. The front page of our local newspaper had a picture of me in my new white shorts, white shirt, white sneakers, and graphite tennis racket with the following headline:

CAN THIS ALEXANDER BE GREAT?

I was the best player, not only at my school but in the district. I'd walk around school and people would high-five me. Even the girl that I liked smiled at me. All of sudden, everybody knew me, wanted to chat and hang out.

The season began and I won my first match. Then I won my second. And before long, I was undefeated. In the district tournament, I wanted nothing more than to redeem the previous year's loss in the finals, to get that first-place trophy. Well, I had the opportunity, and I gave it my all. And I lost again.

But it wasn't over. My teammate and I had made it to the doubles final. Excelling at singles requires individual skill and will. It's almost like singing your favorite song, in tune, on key, for an hour (or two). You keep the ball in the court, don't commit unforced errors, play your game well, don't choke, and you stand a good chance of being victorious.

Playing doubles is all that . . . plus playing in tandem with a partner. Now you have to sing a song with someone else . . . in harmony. It requires two people to think and act as one. Above all, it requires complete trust. My partner, Rob, and I had been winning doubles tournaments all summer, and our games were in sync. The trust and confidence we shared in each other was electric each time we stepped on the court. We ended up winning the district tennis tournament, and I got my first-place trophy.

All along, I'd thought basketball was going to be my sport. My father played it. I was tall. I thought I could ball. To this day, it's my favorite sport to watch. I even wrote a book called *The Crossover*, an homage to hoops, family, and friendship. Turns out, my passion was on a different court. Once I figured that out, I was relentless in my pursuit to excel. I was determined to succeed and be the best player. And, my serve was killer—fast, hard, and tricky. My teammates even gave me a nickname:

"The Big Ace."

Foc

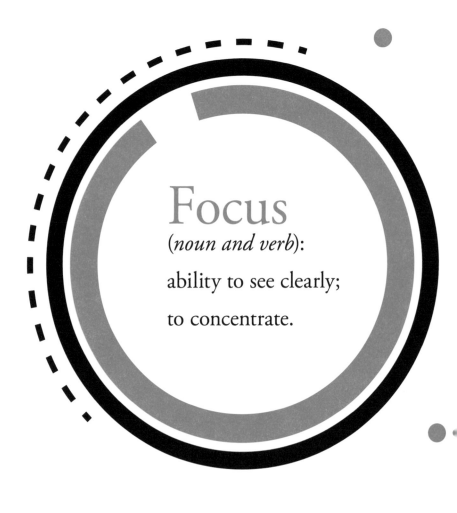

Focus
(*noun and verb*):
ability to see clearly;
to concentrate.

If there is a recipe for success, then one of the main ingredients is focus. And if there is a sport that requires consistent concentration, it's the ninety-minute game of *fútbol*.

On October 23, 1940, in Três Corações, Brazil, the soccer legend Edson Arantes do Nascimento, soon known as Pelé, was born into humble beginnings. It is said his parents, João (Dondinho) Ramos and Dona Celeste, named the future soccer star after history's most famous inventor, Thomas Edison. It seems they knew their son was destined to shine as bright as the sun.

When Pelé was just a little boy, his parents moved to the city of Bauru, where his father was a struggling soccer player. The family was so poor, Dondinho created a soccer ball for Pelé made of a rolled-up sock stuffed with rags and newspaper and tied with a string. Pelé would run through the streets of Bauru barefoot, happily kicking the ball, practicing what would one day become his destiny. He would often skip school to practice in nearby fields. He sold peanuts and shined shoes to earn enough money to buy a real soccer ball. He and his friends formed their own team called the "Shoe-less Ones" because they played barefoot on streets and in vacant lots. These street games gave Pelé the rough edge he needed to eventually compete and be noticed as he perfected his own unique dribbling moves that would pay off later down the road. Pelé was expelled from school in fourth grade because he was caught skipping in favor of playing his beloved sport. He had to take a job as a cobbler's apprentice, making just a couple dollars a day, but it didn't stop him from playing soccer.

97

Pelé was discovered at age eleven by Waldemar de Brito, a former member of the Brazilian national soccer team, who secretly trained Pelé and encouraged him to join a junior football club. At the age

of fifteen, Pelé got permission from his family to leave home and try out for Santos, a top professional soccer team. At the beginning of his second season with Santos, he became a starter and top scorer in the league. In 1957, Pelé was selected for Brazil's national team, and he worked overtime playing for both Santos and Brazil. His dream had become a reality. But sometimes reality becomes even bigger than our dreams.

Before the 1958 World Cup match against Sweden, Pelé had been sidelined for a few games due to a knee injury. Feeling helpless and a bit hopeless, he sat on the bench, encouraging his teammates and summoning the focus to envision the contributions he would make once he was able to return to the pitch. He imagined helping his team to victory. After receiving treatment from doctors, and with the support of his teammates, he insisted that he play, and he was cleared. At just seventeen years old, Pelé, an unknown in the world of soccer, became the youngest athlete to play in the World Cup, leading his team to a 5–2 victory against Sweden.

Over time, he earned the nicknames "Gasoline" for his high, explosive energy, "The Executioner" for his ability to finish a play and score, and "The Black Pearl" because he was a rare and precious gift to his country and the world. The boy who ran through the rough streets of Bauru had his place in history as the greatest soccer player of all time, proving that with heart, focus, commitment, and talent, you can achieve greatness.

I think that in order to get better . . . you have to make goals. Whether you win or whether you're down or tell someone about them, it's important to set goals for yourself in order to achieve any kind of success.

—Abby Wambach, two-time Olympic gold medalist and FIFA Women's World Cup champion.

BEFORE THE GAME
EVEN BEGINS
IMAGINE YOURSELF
MAKING THE TOUGHEST SHOTS
BLOCKING YOUR FIERCEST OPPONENTS
CHANGING THE GAME
AND SEIZING SWEET VICTORY.

FOCUS.
KEEP YOUR EYES
ON THE BALL.
DON'T LOSE SIGHT.
DON'T OVERPLAY.
DON'T GET CROSSED-UP.
KEEP YOUR EYES
ON THE BALL.
FOCUS.

102

Concentration and mental toughness are the margins of victory.

—Bill Russell, **Hall of Fame player/coach, five-time MVP and centerpiece of eleven NBA championships with the Boston Celtics**

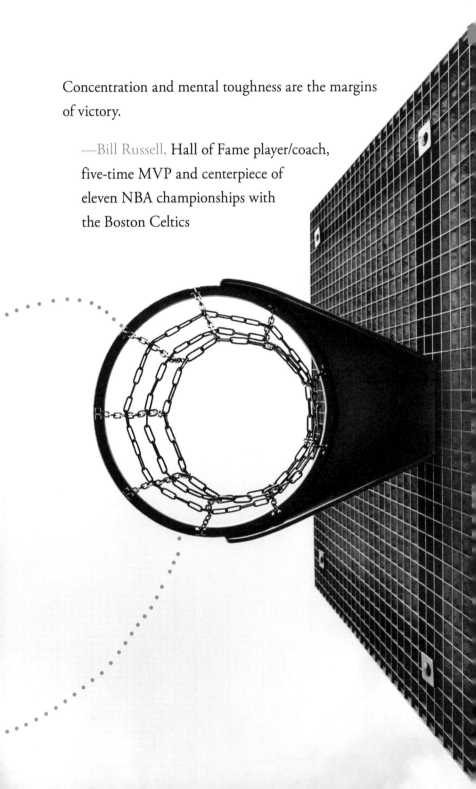

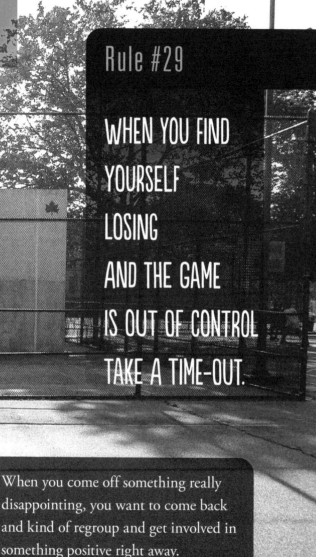

Rule #29

WHEN YOU FIND YOURSELF LOSING AND THE GAME IS OUT OF CONTROL TAKE A TIME-OUT.

When you come off something really disappointing, you want to come back and kind of regroup and get involved in something positive right away.

—Andy Roddick, number one tennis player (ATP rankings), U.S. Open champion

THERE IS NO SINGLE FORMULA FOR WINNING BUT YOU MUST HAVE A GAME PLAN.

I never worry about the problem. I worry about the solution.

—Shaquille O'Neal, four-time NBA champion with the Los Angeles Lakers and the Miami Heat, fifteen-time NBA all-star

108

WHEN YOU GET BENCHED,
STEP YOUR MENTAL GAME UP,
GET YOURSELF READY TO RETURN.

YOU MIGHT FOUL UP,
BUT DON'T FOUL OUT.

109

Excellence is the gradual result of always
striving to do better.

—Pat Riley, five-time NBA champion
head coach of the Los Angeles Lakers
and the Miami Heat

Every time you fall down,
it gives you an opportunity to question
yourself, question your integrity. . . . It's not about
the actual failure itself—it's how you respond to it.

—Abby Wambach, two-time Olympic gold medalist
and FIFA Women's World Cup champion

Rule #32

SOMETIMES
YOU HAVE TO
LEAN BACK
A LITTLE
AND
FADE AWAY
TO GET
THE BEST
SHOT.

111

IF YOU'RE OFF-BALANCE
OR DON'T FEEL COMFORTABLE
NEVER RUSH YOUR SHOT.

KICK THE BALL OUT.
RESTART.
TAKE THE TIME

YOU NEED
TO GET A
BETTER POSITION.

I try to do the right thing at the right time. They may just be little things, but usually they make the difference between winning and losing.

–Kareem Abdul-Jabbar, six-time NBA champion with the Los Angeles Lakers and the Milwaukee Bucks, six-time MVP

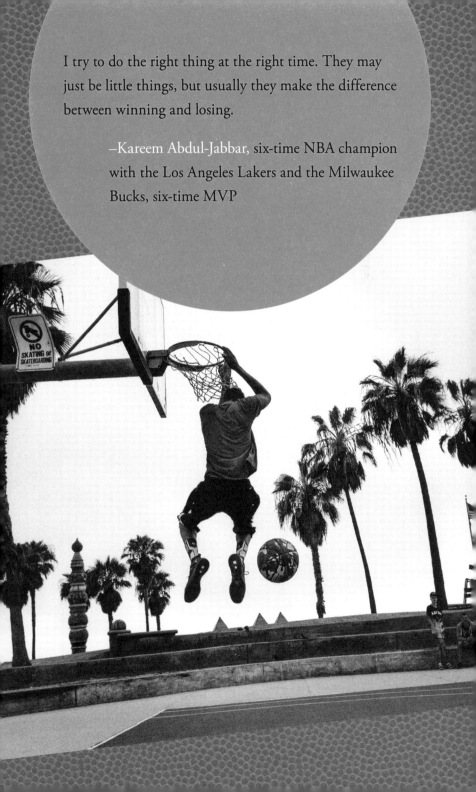

Rule #34

THE ROAD
TO
WINNING
THE BIG CHAMPIONSHIPS
IS FILLED WITH
BUMPS AND DIPS.

The harder you work and the more prepared you are for something, you're going to be able to persevere through anything.

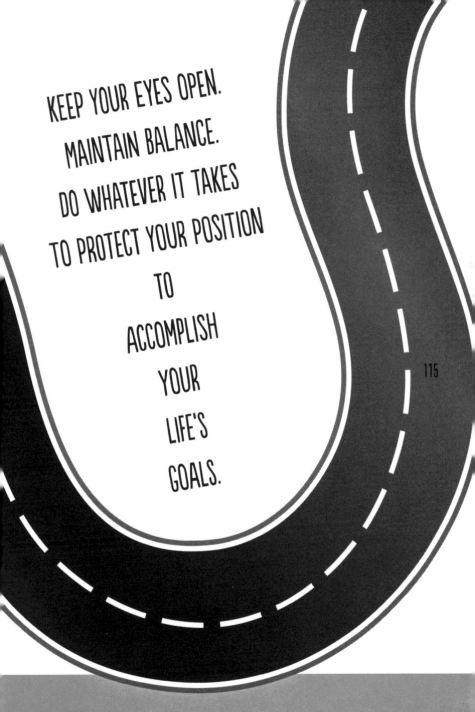

KEEP YOUR EYES OPEN.
MAINTAIN BALANCE.
DO WHATEVER IT TAKES
TO PROTECT YOUR POSITION
TO
ACCOMPLISH
YOUR
LIFE'S
GOALS.

115

—Carli Lloyd, two-time Olympic gold medalist, FIFA Women's
World Cup champion, and 2015 FIFA Women's Player of the Year

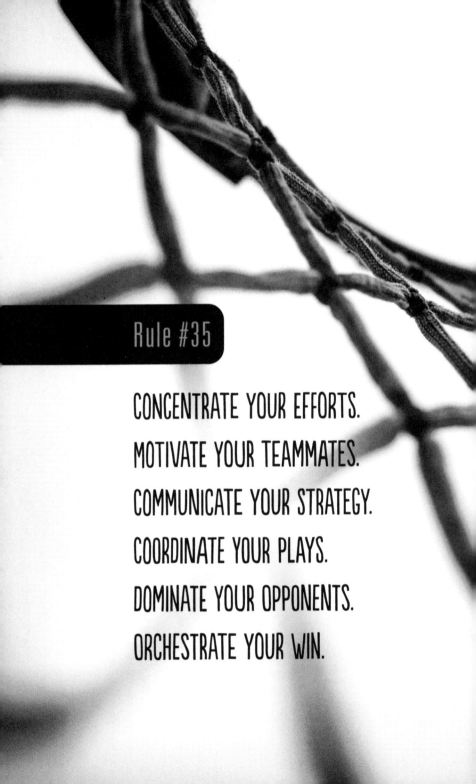

Rule #35

CONCENTRATE YOUR EFFORTS.
MOTIVATE YOUR TEAMMATES.
COMMUNICATE YOUR STRATEGY.
COORDINATE YOUR PLAYS.
DOMINATE YOUR OPPONENTS.
ORCHESTRATE YOUR WIN.

There is no magic to achievement. It's really about hard work, choices, and persistence.

—Michelle Obama, **First Lady of the United States of America**

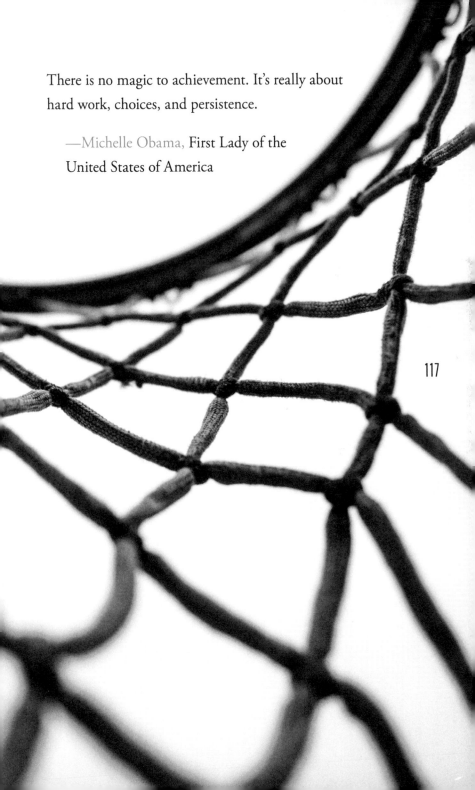

IF YOU'RE THE POINT GUARD
YOU HAVE A SPLIT SECOND
TO READ THE COURT
ACT SWIFTLY
AND SET THE PLAY
THAT COULD CHANGE
THE GAME.

If you have a chance to accomplish something that will make things better for people coming behind you, and you don't do that, you are wasting your time on this earth.

—Roberto Clemente, two-time World Series champion and twelve-time MLB all-star with the Pittsburgh Pirates

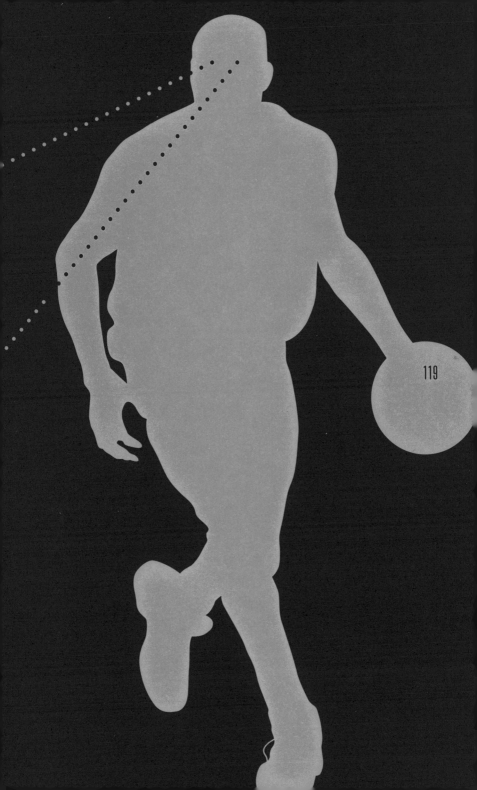

119

STARTING
WITH A SIMPLE MOVE
LIKE A LAY-UP
CAN BUILD CONFIDENCE
AS YOU MOVE
THROUGH THE HARD SCREENS
AND TOUGH CHALLENGES
ON YOUR WAY
TO THE GOAL.

121

A surplus of effort could overcome a deficit of confidence.

—Sonia Sotomayor, **U.S. Supreme Court justice**

THE FIRST STEP
IN ACHIEVING
POSITIVE RESULTS
IS PLANNING
TO ACHIEVE
POSITIVE
RESULTS.

THE SECOND STEP
IS ACTUALLY WORKING
THE PLAN.

You have to expect things of yourself before you can do them.

—Michael Jordan, six-time NBA champion with the Chicago Bulls, five-time MVP

IT'S OKAY TO
TAKE TIME OUT
SLOW DOWN
HUDDLE
BREATHE
REGROUP
REFOCUS
RESTART.

124

All great achievements require time.

—Maya Angelou, acclaimed poet and author
of *I Know Why the Caged Bird Sings*

4th Quarter

Team

work

and Resilience

Teamwork *(noun)*:

the combined
action of
a group
of people,
especially
when
effective.

X

Resilience *(noun)*:

the ability to
recover quickly
from difficulty;
toughness.

130

If you've never seen Venus and Serena Williams play against each other, go watch the 2000 Wimbledon Finals or the 2002 French Open Finals. *Stunning, powerful,* and *tense* are the best words to describe it. When they first played each other in 1999, Venus beat her younger sister. But, later that year, Serena bounced back and defeated Venus. I watched all these matches, and many more, and their resilience is awe-inspiring. They simply never give up.

Venus and Serena were the youngest two of five sisters born to Richard and Oracene (Brandi) Williams, and they spent much of their childhood in and around Compton, California. Richard was a superfan of tennis and was determined to help his daughters learn the finer points of the game. He put rackets in all his daughters' hands, teaching them how to power serve and rally and volley.

The girls were homeschooled by their mother, and practiced their tennis skills with their father for hours every day. They didn't wear hip and cool tennis outfits or fancy sneakers, because they couldn't afford them. So they practiced in their jeans on Compton courts, which had potholes and missing nets, under the

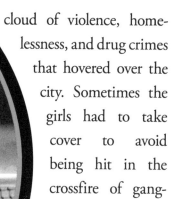

cloud of violence, homelessness, and drug crimes that hovered over the city. Sometimes the girls had to take cover to avoid being hit in the crossfire of gang-related activity.

There weren't just the dangers of Compton, though—there were the emotional challenges the girls faced at games in other cities and places where they stood out as being different. They were often the only African Americans at a tournament. In order to prepare Venus and Serena for the harsh realities of playing tennis in front of racist crowds, Richard sometimes paid other children to yell out rude and demeaning comments to his daughters during their practices. Venus and Serena developed focus and a thick skin for the long, arduous journey to tennis stardom.

At seven years old, Venus started receiving attention from tennis elites such as Pete Sampras and John McEnroe, both of whom encouraged her to keep playing. By age ten, she was already ranked the number one player in the Under-12 division in Southern California. *Sports Illustrated* and *Tennis* magazine wrote stories about the young tennis star from the dangerous streets of Compton. Serena was not far behind, racking up accolades with the same distinction. Their hard work paid off. When they finally turned pro, Venus would go on to win nine Grand Slam championships, and Serena a whopping twenty-one. Together, they also accomplished something that very few players have done: The sisters teamed up to win thirteen Grand Slam doubles titles, including the prestigious Golden Slam—winning an Olympic gold medal and all four Grand Slam titles in their career.

From the tough courts of Compton to the world stage of tennis, the Williams sisters—models of raw, undeterred resilience—have broken barriers and changed the game of tennis forever. And they did it together. No matter whether they are playing against each other or cheering the other on during a match, the Williams sisters understand the value and importance of having someone in your corner, of supporting and encouraging each other. As Venus says, "My first job is big sister and I take that very seriously."

Who's got *your* back?

Rule #40

REAL TEAMMATES
CHEER YOU ON
IN VICTORY
AND EVEN
IN DEFEAT.

The strength of the team is each individual member. The strength of each member is the team.

—Phil Jackson, eleven-time NBA championship–winning coach with the Chicago Bulls and the Los Angeles Lakers

A GREAT TEAM
HAS A GOOD SCORER
WITH A TEAMMATE
WHO'S ON POINT
AND READY
TO ASSIST.

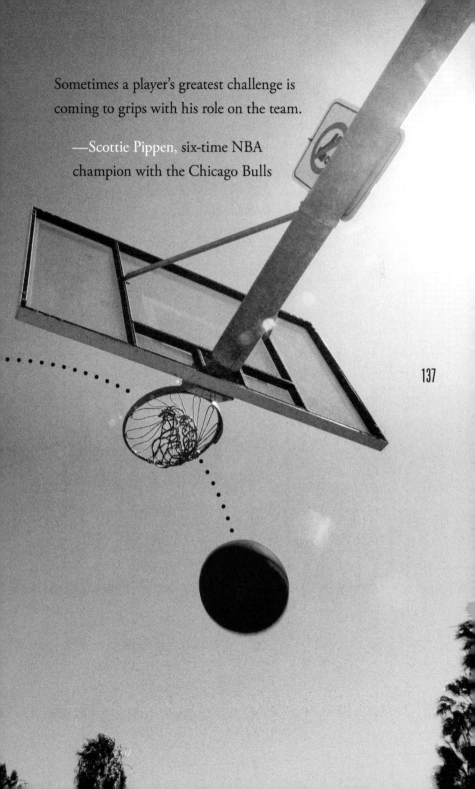

Sometimes a player's greatest challenge is
coming to grips with his role on the team.

—Scottie Pippen, six-time NBA
champion with the Chicago Bulls

137

BE UNSELFISH.
SHARE THE BALL.

WORK TOGETHER.
WIN TOGETHER.

The most important measure of how good a game I played was how much better I'd made my teammates play.

—Bill Russell, Hall of Fame player/coach, five-time MVP and centerpiece of eleven NBA championships with the Boston Celtics

139

WINNING HAPPENS WHEN FIVE PLAYERS ON THE COURT PLAY WITH ONE HEART.

Talent wins games, but teammates and intelligence win championships.

—Michael Jordan, six-time NBA champion with the Chicago Bulls, five-time MVP

TEAMMATES ARE LIKE FAMILY, CELEBRATING WINS, CONSOLING LOSSES, ALWAYS A NET TIED TOGETHER.

142

Surround yourself with only people who are going to lift you higher.

—Oprah Winfrey, studio executive, producer, talk show host, actress, philanthropist

A LOSS IS INEVITABLE, LIKE RAIN IN SPRING. TRUE CHAMPIONS LEARN TO DANCE THROUGH THE STORM.

144

It's what you get from games you lose that is extremely important.

—Pat Riley, five-time NBA champion head coach of the Los Angeles Lakers and the Miami Heat

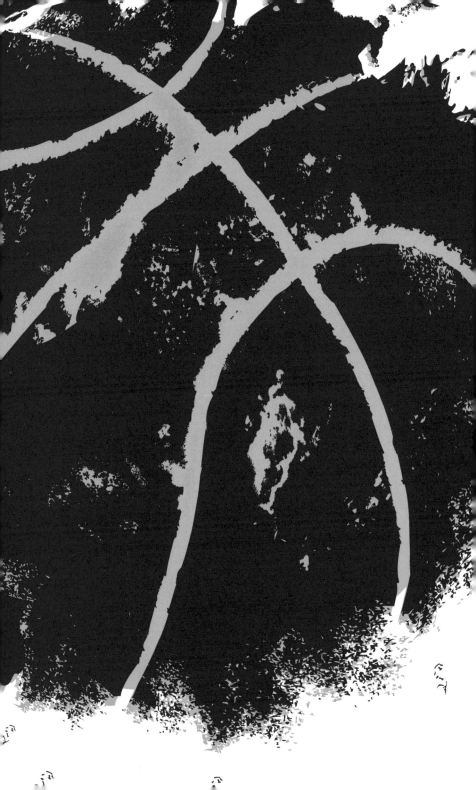

Rule #46

YOU TURN THE BALL OVER?
LET IT GO.

YOU MISS A BIG SHOT?
LET IT GO.

LEARN FROM YOUR MISTAKES.
MOVE FORWARD.

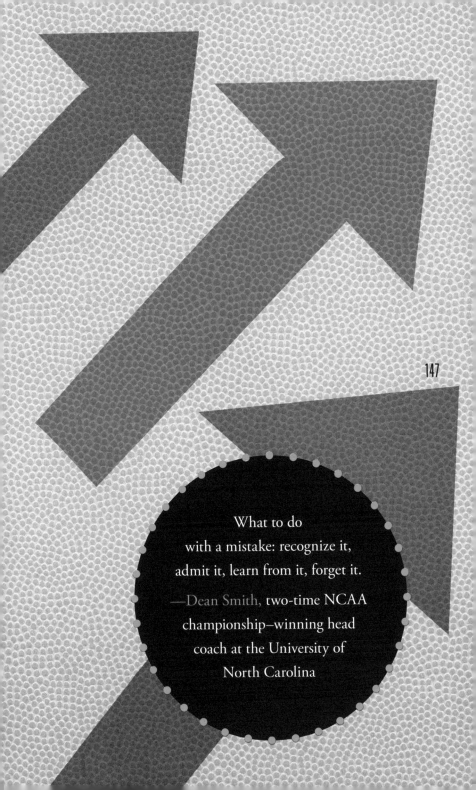

147

What to do
with a mistake: recognize it,
admit it, learn from it, forget it.

—Dean Smith, two-time NCAA
championship–winning head
coach at the University of
North Carolina

148

Rule #47

IF YOU MISS
ENOUGH OF LIFE'S
FREE THROWS
YOU WILL PAY
IN THE END.

149

Mistakes are a fact of life. It is the response to the error that counts.

—Nikki Giovanni, acclaimed poet, author of *Ego-Tripping and Other Poems for Young People*

150

WHEN YOUR SHOT
GETS BLOCKED
DON'T FEAR.
YOU'VE GOT TO GET
THE BALL BACK
REESTABLISH POSITION
AND PLAN
YOUR NEXT MOVE.

I learned that courage was not the absence of fear, but the triumph over it. The brave man is not he who does not feel afraid, but he who conquers that fear.

—Nelson Mandela, president of South Africa, Nobel Peace Prize winner

151

Persistence can change failure into extraordinary achievement.

—Matt Biondi, U.S. Olympic swimmer, eight-time gold medalist

DRIBBLE FAKE SHOOT MISS
DRIBBLE FAKE SHOOT MISS
DRIBBLE FAKE SHOOT MISS
DRIBBLE FAKE SHOOT SWISH!

153

154

LOSING
IS AN OPPORTUNITY
TO GET BETTER,
TO LEARN
WHAT TO DO
TO WIN.

155

We may encounter many defeats but we must
not be defeated.

—Maya Angelou, acclaimed poet and
author of *I Know Why the Caged Bird Sings*

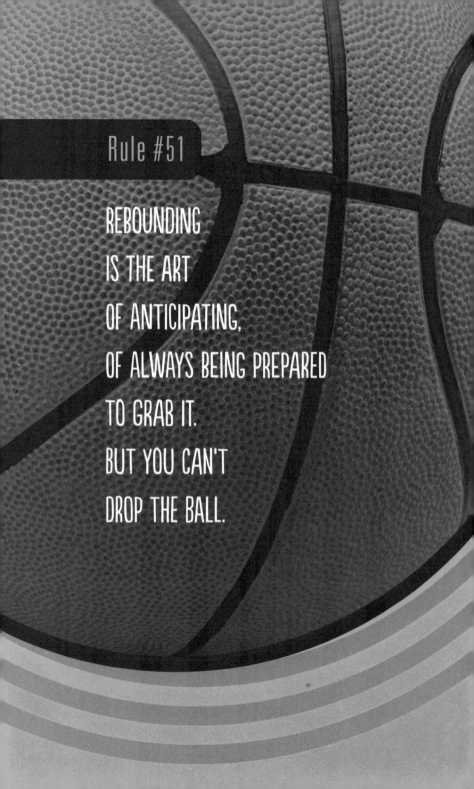

Rule #51

REBOUNDING
IS THE ART
OF ANTICIPATING,
OF ALWAYS BEING PREPARED
TO GRAB IT.
BUT YOU CAN'T
DROP THE BALL.

Like life, basketball is messy and unpredictable. It has its way with you, no matter how hard you try to control it. The trick is to experience each moment with a clear mind and open heart. When you do that, the game and life will take care of itself.

—Phil Jackson, eleven-time NBA championship–winning coach with the Chicago Bulls and the Los Angeles Lakers

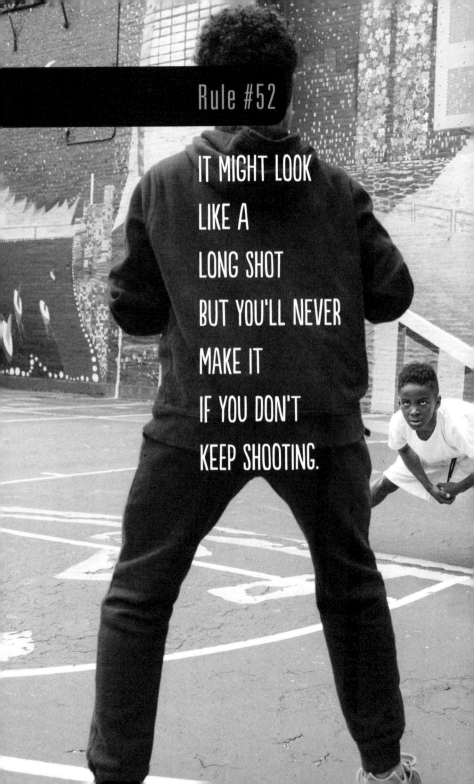

Rule #52

IT MIGHT LOOK
LIKE A
LONG SHOT
BUT YOU'LL NEVER
MAKE IT
IF YOU DON'T
KEEP SHOOTING.

159

You miss 100 percent of the shots you don't take.

—Wayne Gretzky, four-time Stanley Cup winner, recognized as the greatest hockey player of all time by many sportswriters

Overtime

162

Tenacity (*noun*):
determination, persistence.

When Lew Alcindor started playing basketball in college for UCLA, the NCAA officials felt that he was too dominant a player—because at seven feet, two inches he could dunk the ball too easily (not to mention way too FIERCELY). They felt he would be unstoppable. So in 1967 they changed the rules to forbid dunking in college games. This was called the "Alcindor Rule." Can you imagine the game of basketball without dunking? No way the NCAA's March Madness or the NBA would be so popular without Michael Jordan tongue wagging and soaring to the hoop for a *dunkalicious* slam!

As a result of the rule, Alcindor developed a great hook shot, which he used effectively during his playing days in college and the NBA to win three consecutive NCAA championships and six NBA championships. Lew Alcindor did not let the new no-dunking rule change thwart him. He *rebounded*, simply made up his own rule, and created the most lethal shot in hoops history—the hook. Shortly after he started playing professional basketball, he changed his name to Kareem Abdul-Jabbar. The

Alcindor rule was rescinded in 1975, and players were allowed to dunk again.

From Kareem Abdul-Jabaar to Steph Curry (who many college coaches said was too small to play for their team); from Venus and Serena to Tamika Catchings—the ten-year WNBA all-star, MVP, and WNBA champion who is also deaf—there are tales of athletes who have defied the odds and achieved greatness. And they've all had a few things in common: they know the rules and never give up! And *you* shouldn't either. I'm not saying it's easy, but I am saying that the hard work, grit, and *say yes* attitude is well worth it in the end. Just remember:

BE TENACIOUS.

BELIEVE IN YOURSELF EVEN WHEN IT SEEMS THAT NO ONE ELSE DOES.

SOMETIMES YOU HAVE TO CHOOSE YOUR OWN MOVES.

SURROUND YOURSELF WITH THE RIGHT TEAM, WITH PEOPLE WHO SUPPORT YOU, WHO ARE EQUALLY—IF NOT MORE—PASSIONATE AND AMBITIOUS.

OWN YOUR POSITION,
CONTROL IT, MOVE YOUR FEET, ROTATE, PUT YOUR NAME ON THE BALL.

CREATE YOUR OWN PLAY.

HONOR THE ONES WHO'VE COME BEFORE YOU.

HONOR THE GREATNESS
THAT IS YOU.

PRACTICE...

...FACE DEFEAT.

REBOUND.

EXPECT TO WIN.

WIN.

WALK THROUGH UNFAMILIAR

DOORS.

KNOW THE RULES.

MASTER THE RULES.

SAY YES

TO THE POSSIBILITY

OF SOMETIMES

MAKING UP

YOUR OWN.

...RULES!

169

KWAME ALEXANDER is a poet, educator, and *New York Times* bestselling author of thirty-six books, including *Swing*; *Becoming Muhammad Ali*, coauthored with James Patterson; *Rebound*, which was shortlisted for the prestigious UK Carnegie Medal; the Caldecott Medal–winning and Newbery Honor–winning picture book, *The Undefeated*, illustrated by Kadir Nelson; and his Newbery Medal–winning middle grade novel, *The Crossover*. A regular contributor to NPR's *Morning Edition*, Kwame is the recipient of numerous awards, including the Lee Bennett Hopkins Poetry Award, the Coretta Scott King Author Honor, three NAACP Image Award nominations, and the 2017 inaugural Pat Conroy Legacy Award. In 2018, he opened the Barbara E. Alexander Memorial Library and Health Clinic in Ghana, as a part of LEAP for Ghana, an international literacy program he cofounded. He is the writer and executive producer of *The Crossover* TV series on Disney+.

Also by Kwame Alexander

THE CROSSOVER

In this Newbery Medal–winning middle grade novel in verse, twelve-year-old twin basketball stars Josh and Jordan wrestle with highs and lows on and off the court.

Newbery Medal Winner
Coretta Scott King Honor Award Winner
A *New York Times* Bestseller

"A beautifully measured novel of life and lines."
—*New York Times Book Review*

"Alexander's at the top of his poetic game in this taut, complex tale of the crossover from brash, vulnerable boy to young adult." —*Washington Post*

BOOKED

In this middle grade novel in verse, soccer, family, love, and friendship take center stage as twelve-year-old Nick learns the power of words, wrestles with problems at home, stands up to a bully, and tries to impress the girl of his dreams.

A *New York Times* Bestseller
National Book Award Longlist Nominee

"To pick up *Booked* is to find yourself turning page after page, swept along as Nick spills out his story." —*New York Times Book Review*

ABOUT THE PHOTOGRAPHER

THAI NEAVE is a former SportsCenter anchor for ESPN and now works as a freelance photographer and director. He currently resides between New York and Los Angeles. Follow his work at shootinghoops.com.